Bo the Funny Log

Om KIDZ
An imprint of Om Books International

Om Books International

Reprinted in 2021

Corporate & Editorial Office
A-12, Sector 64, Noida 201 301
Uttar Pradesh, India
Phone: +91 120 477 4100
Email: editorial@ombooks.com
Website: www.ombooksinternational.com

Sales Office
107, Ansari Road, Darya Ganj
New Delhi 110 002, India
Phone: +91 11 4000 9000
Email: sales@ombooks.com

© Om Books International 2016

ISBN: 978-93-85273-76-6

Printed in India

10 9 8 7 6 5 4 3

Bob and the Funny Log

I'm all set to read

Puste your
photograph here

My name is

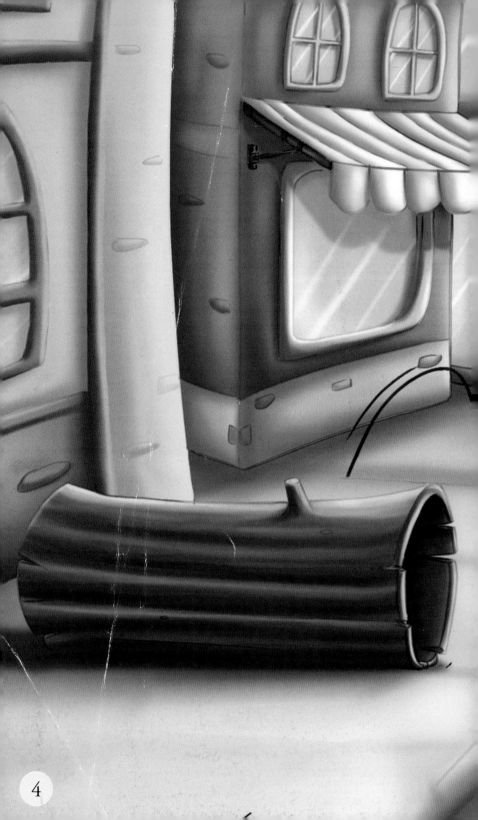

All of a sudden, they get **lost** in the **fog**.

"Woof! Woof! Woof!"
Bob follows the **dog's** bark
and finds the **hopping log.**

Bop! Bop! Bop!
The **log hops** as **Bob** and
the **dog** try to catch it.

"Phew! It is so **hot**!" says **Bob** as he **spots** a **pond**.

The **hopping log** finally comes to a **stop** at the **pond**.

The **dog** runs ahead of **Bob** and sniffs the **log**.

A curious **Bob** carefully **prods** the **log** with a stick he finds near the **pond**.

Hop! Hop! Hop!
Suddenly, a **lot** of **frogs** jump out from inside the **log**.

"An army of **hopping frogs** was carrying the **log** all along!" says **Bob**.

Know your phonic words

These words have the short "o" sound in them.

Bob	fog
off	hot
job	spot
odd	pond
log	stop
hop	prod
hopping	frog
on	lot
jog	bop
dog	
lost	